My Rat is a Hero

FRANK RODGERS

MACDONALD YOUNG BOOKS

LEABHARLANNA CHONTAE NA GAILLIMHE
(GALWAY COUNTY LIBRARIES)

EW

Acc. No....J111 588..... Class No.........................

Date of Return	Date of Return	Date of Return

Books are on loan for 21 days from date of issue.

Fines for overdue books: 10p for each week or portion of a week plus cost of postage incurred in recovery.

Chapter One

The little creature from the planet *Whee* just didn't get it. He scratched the tuft of hair on the top of his head and looked at me curiously with his pink eyes.

"You're going to *where*, pardner?"

I sighed and sat down on the edge of my bed. Ratso watched me from his spaceship parked on top of my table. The alien who had crash-landed in my garden not long ago obviously didn't know too much about Earth, I thought.

"The seaside, Ratso," I said again. "Sun, sand, sea and all that."

Ratso leant on the hatch of his spaceship and regarded me with a frown.

"I know what sand is, pardner," he said in his favourite cowboy accent. "We've got plenty of that on our planet. And I know what the sun is. It's that big, burning star I flew past on my way here. But what the heck is *sea*?"

"It's water, Ratso," I explained. "A *huge* amount of water like a gigantic lake. Only it's salty."

The little alien's eyes lit up.

"Yeah! Now I remember! I saw it on a TV programme I picked up in my spaceship on the way here. It covers most of your planet and there are some mighty strange things in it, like – sharks!"

"Not at our seaside," I said with a grin.

Ratso climbed out of his spaceship and jumped down on to the table. He had been checking to see how much damage had been done and wiped his little pink hands on an oily rag.

"*Whee* is pretty dry," he said. "We get our water from wells so I'd be mighty interested in seeing one of those seas of yours."

"I'm afraid you can't, Ratso," I said. "I told you. It's a class trip."

"And I'm going with you," said Ratso.

"Oh, no you're not," I replied grimly. "The last time you visited my class it was a disaster!"

"Oh, yes I am," said Ratso defiantly.

"Oh, no you are most certainly not!" I said right back. "That is a definite no-no! No, no, no, no, no. Get it?"

The little alien folded his arms and scowled. He didn't reply and I congratulated myself that for once I had got my own way by being firm.

I really should have known better.

Chapter Two

"*Hai-yaaa!*" Mum gave the loaf a vicious karate chop with the heel of her hand. The bread disintegrated in a burst of crumbs as if it had been hit by a bomb.

"I wish you wouldn't practise your martial arts in the kitchen, Sue," sighed Dad. "Can't you see I'm trying to conduct Beethoven's Fifth Symphony?" He took off his headphones and switched off the cassette. "And why don't you use the bread knife?" he complained, looking at the lumpy mess on the worktop. "That's the third loaf you've ruined this week."

Mum sighed and swept the shattered bits of bread to one side. "I'll get the hang of the karate chop one of these days," she said and opened a bag of rolls. "Cheese and pickle all right for your lunch, Gary?" she asked.

"Fine, Mum," I replied. "But I'm in a bit of a hurry. The bus leaves the school gates in ten minutes."

"Don't worry," Mum said. "Your lunch will be ready in two ticks." She began buttering the rolls. "How's my little darling Ratso, this morning?" she asked with a soppy smile.

Dad rolled his eyes and muttered, "Little pest, you mean."

I had managed to keep Ratso's true identity a secret from Mum and Dad so they believed that Ratso was just an ordinary pet rat. Mum thought he was cute and cuddly and Dad thought he was a pain in the neck.

The only other person who knew that Ratso was an alien teacher was my friend, Bobby – and he was always having trouble keeping it to himself.

"He's fine, Mum," I said and put my rucksack on my chair. "He was still sleeping under a pile of straw in his cage when I left my room." I almost added, "He's in a huff because he can't come on the school trip," but stopped myself just in time.

"I'll go up and see him later," said Mum. "I hope he talks to me."

I gave a start then realized that what Mum meant by 'talk' was the funny rat-like squeaks and chirps that Ratso made when he spoke his alien language. I understood them because the little creature had given me an earpiece translator to wear, but everybody else just thought they were normal rat noises.

Mum wrapped up the rolls, put them in my rucksack and zipped up the top.

"What have you got in here, Gary?" she said with a smile as she lifted the bag off the chair. "Feels heavy."

"Just my stuff for the beach, Mum," I replied as I swung the rucksack on to my shoulder. I counted the items off on my fingers. "Towel, swimming trunks, camera and my old trainers and ball for playing footie on the beach. Just the usual stuff," I said with a grin. "No surprises there."

I couldn't have been more wrong.

Chapter Three

Mr Anderton checked with Mrs Murphy, the other teacher, and made a note on his clipboard. "Right," he said, "Everyone's here." He tapped the bus driver on the shoulder and smiled. "Time to go, Mr Peters. The annual class trip can now commence!"

As the bus moved away from the school gates everybody cheered. I was sitting beside Bobby and he punched the air in delight.

"Yes!" he cried. "I love the seaside!"

Derek 'The Pain' Butane, the class bully, leaned over the back of our seat and smirked.

"Brought your little bucket and spade have you, Bobby? Going to build a poxy little sand-castle?"

He looked at me and glowered. "And as for you, Smithy," he hissed. "Just watch out on the beach." He stuck his fingers up on either side of his head and let some spit drool out of the corner of his mouth. "Derek the sea monster might get you. Ha-haa!"

He sat back in his seat beside his two pals, Kev and Jimmy, and snorted with laughter.

I sighed. Every term The Pain picked on someone and this term it was my turn.

"Just ignore him," whispered Bobby. "He'll forget about it soon enough."

But he didn't.

The Pain kept up a running commentary about what was going to happen to me when we got to the beach. I took Bobby's advice and totally ignored him but after a while he began to get annoyed. Spying my rucksack on the luggage rack he reached up and yanked it down.

"Let's see if Smithy's got anything good to eat in here," he sniggered. He unzipped the top and thrust his hand inside.

I whirled round in my seat angrily.

"Give that back!" I shouted. I was about to reach over the back of the seat when The Pain let out a sudden yelp and pulled his hand out of the bag.

"Ow!" he squealed. "There's something horrible in there! It bit me!"

I wrenched the rucksack away from him just as Ratso's head appeared from the folds of my towel.

"Howdy, pardner," he said. "Are we at the seaside yet?"

I was speechless.

"It's Gary's rat!" cried Sophie Miller from the seat across the aisle.

"Yo, Gary!" yelled Sam Lafferty in approval.

J711,588

Suddenly everybody on the bus wanted a look and the whole class crowded round laughing and pointing.

"He's so cute, Gary!" laughed Gemma Price.

"I am *not* cute!" cried Ratso. "I'm a teacher just like your Mr Anderton."

"Listen to it!" laughed Naz Patel. "It's cool!"

"What's going on?" demanded Mr Anderton, pushing his way through the throng. "Get back to your seats everyone!"

His eyes popped when he saw Ratso. "What's that doing here?" he cried. "Why on earth did you bring your rat along?"

"I… I didn't, sir," I said limply.

"It's a stowaway," Bobby chortled.

"That poxy rat bit me!" yelled The Pain. "It should be put down!"

"Calm yourself, Derek," said Mr Anderton and grabbed The Pain's hands. "Let's see." He turned over and studied them carefully. "There are no marks, Derek," he said. "Are you sure you were bitten?"

The Pain glared at his hands, annoyed that the teacher was right.

"Felt like it," he mumbled.

Somebody whispered, "Big baby," and The Pain whirled round with a ferocious scowl.

"Who said that?" he snarled. "I'll rearrange their features!"

"That's enough!" snapped Mr Anderton. "If I have any trouble from you, Derek, you will stay with me and Mrs Murphy all day."

He turned to me and pointed to Ratso.

"The last thing I want running loose on this trip is a pet rat. There are thirty-two of you in this class and that's quite enough of a responsibility."

"I am not a pet, gosh durn it!" Ratso yelled, waving his arms around. "I'm a teacher just like you!"

Mr Anderton frowned and peered at Ratso. "Noisy, isn't it?" he said. "And it's behaving rather oddly for a rat."

25

"That's because it's not a rat, sir," Bobby blurted out without thinking. "It's a creature from outer— ow!" he yelped as I dug him desperately in the ribs.

"Mongolia, sir," I said quickly. "Er… Bobby means that Ratso is a creature from Outer Mongolia." I glared at Bobby and dug him in the ribs again. "Don't you, Bobby?"

"Ow! Well… yeah…" said Bobby, realizing he had nearly given Ratso's secret away in a mad moment. "That's right, sir. Er… Ratso's a cross between a rat and a very small Outer Mongolian yak. He really should be called a *yat*."

Mr Anderton looked doubtful.

"Whatever it is, Gary," he said. "Keep it under control. Or *else*." He turned and went back to the front of the bus.

"I'll get you!" hissed The Pain when the teacher sat down again. "Just you wait!"

I groaned and looked at Ratso. This trip was shaping up to be another disaster.

Chapter Four

It was perfect seaside weather when we arrived at the beach. The sun shone in a blue sky and sparkled brightly on the blue water. Some of the class took off their shoes and dug their toes into the warm sand.

"Oooh, brilliant," cried Sophie Miller.

"Heaven," sighed Fiona Pettigrew.

"Garbage!" grunted Derek Butane. He kicked a spray of sand at me and slouched off towards the amusement arcade followed by Jimmy and Kev.

The sand splattered all over my back, spraying Ratso as he popped his head out of the rucksack.

"Ptcha!" he spluttered, spitting out sand and wiping his face. "Doggone it! Who did that?!"

"Derek 'The Pain' Butane," I muttered as I brushed the little alien down. "He's out to get me."

"Not if I get him first," Ratso murmured darkly.

"Please, Ratso," I begged. "Don't do anything *weird*. OK? I'd rather deal with this myself if you don't mind."

"Suit yourself, pardner," said the little creature. He pointed to the water. "Is that the sea?"

I nodded.

"Sure is big," mused Ratso. He looked along the beach. "What's that place with all the coloured lights?"

"It's a fun-fair," I replied.

"I can see horses!" Ratso cried. "Yahoo! Looks like a rodeo! Will the cowboys be there?"

Ratso had a thing about cowboys. He had wanted to be one ever since he had picked up his first TV western on his way to Earth.

"Sorry to disappoint you, Ratso," I said, "but there are no cowboys. And those horses are wooden. They're on a roundabout."

"A roundabout?"

"Yes. The horses just go round and round."

Ratso was amazed. "That's all they do?"

"Yes."

The little alien shook his head. "You sure do have some strange ideas about having fun on this planet," he said. "Yes, siree."

I heard shouts and laughter and saw that most of my class were in the sea, larking about. Pulling my towel from the rucksack I began to change.

"I'm going for a swim, Ratso," I said. "I'll only be gone about ten minutes. OK?"

"But I want to have a close look at that sea thing!"

"Tell you what," I said and pointed to some boats. "I'll take you out on one of those later. You can have an extra close look then, all right?"

Ratso peered at the boats doubtfully then shrugged. "Sure thing, pardner," he said and climbed back into the rucksack. "I'll have myself a quick sleep till then."

I joined my friends and had such a good time messing about in the shallows that I forgot all about Ratso. When I remembered I asked Bobby to look at his waterproof watch and found I had been away for half an hour.

I sprinted up the beach to apologize for being away so long. But when I reached the spot where I'd left him my heart leapt. My towel and other clothes were there but my rucksack was gone.

Quickly, I put on my T-shirt and shorts and frantically looked left and right along the beach, but there was no sign of either it or Ratso.

Chapter Five

"Lost something, have you?"

I looked up and saw Derek Butane sitting on the sea wall at the top of the beach with his two pals. He was grinning nastily and slurping a huge ice-cream cone.

"A poxy pet, maybe?"

I ran towards him, fists clenched.

"What have you done with my rucksack?" I yelled.

"Me?" The Pain said, looking hurt. "Nothing to do with me if you forget where you put your rucksack, Smithy." He turned first to Jimmy then to Kev and smirked. "What do you think, lads?"

Jimmy and Kev sniggered.

"Nothing to do with you, Del," they said.

"I left it on my towel!" I shouted. "You moved it!"

The Pain sneered at me. "Oh, yeah? Prove it."

I nearly grabbed the ice-cream cone and pushed it into his face but the worry that Ratso was lost somewhere stopped me having it out with Derek there and then.

I looked round for Mr Anderton but he was nowhere to be seen. Knowing that The Pain would never tell me where he had hidden my rucksack I turned on my heel and rushed off along the beach to look for it.

"Ha-haa!" laughed The Pain. "Little Smithy's running away. Maybe he'll cry. Boo-hoo!"

Jimmy and Kev joined in his laughter.

I hardly heard their taunts as my mind was doing cartwheels worrying about Ratso.

Although the little creature was a fully grown adult *Wheesh* and believed he could take care of himself on Earth, I knew he couldn't. Everyone here thought he was just a rat and treated him like a pet, so he needed me to look after him. I didn't do a very good job of that, I thought, leaving him alone on the beach when someone like The Pain was around.

As I tried to think where Ratso might be it occurred to me that Derek might have put the rucksack somewhere in the fun-fair. I had noticed Jimmy and Kev glancing in that direction, nudging each other and grinning. The fun-fair would certainly be full of good hiding places, so I made a beeline for it.

Bobby caught up with me just as I reached
the fun-fair and I quickly explained what had
happened.

"Why don't we just call for Ratso?" he
suggested. "I mean, as an alien, he's probably
got super-sensitive hearing. I'm sure he'd find
a way of letting you know where he is."

"That's what I'm afraid of," I replied. "He
might get all excited and turn into a lion or
something and then what would we do? No.
I think I'll try and do this quietly if you don't
mind."

"Suit yourself," said Bobby.

We split up and searched different parts of the fun-fair but when we met up again ten minutes later neither of us had found the rucksack. Then we met Naz Patel at the Hoopla stall and he told us he'd seen The Pain earlier over by the Big Wheel.

Bobby and I rushed over there straight away and began our search all over again. But five minutes later we were still searching.

"No luck," I groaned and flopped down on a bench beside the pay booth.

Bobby sat down beside me and looked up at the Big Wheel.

Suddenly he gripped my shoulder.

"Gary! Look!" he cried hoarsely. "Up there!"

I looked in the direction he was pointing and gasped. My rucksack was hanging from a piece of metal that stuck out from the outer rim of the Big Wheel.

The wheel was moving and, as I watched in horror, one of the straps came loose and the rucksack began to swing from side to side.

As the wheel took the bag higher the swinging motion became more violent.

"Poor Ratso!" I yelped. "If the bag falls he's a goner!"

"I'll go and tell the man in the booth!" cried Bobby and turned to run.

"Oh no!" I gasped.

Bobby stopped in his tracks and looked up. The bag had reached the top of the Big Wheel, about twenty metres in the air, and we could see quite plainly that the remaining strap was starting to slip off too...

Chapter Six

Bobby and I stood, holding our breaths, willing the bag not to fall. We watched, agonized, as the wheel moved on. The strap stopped slipping and we froze, hoping against hope that it would hold.

For a moment it looked as if Ratso was safe
after all, then suddenly the bag jerked, the
strap came off the metal projection and the
rucksack fell into space. Mouths open in
horror we watched as, seemingly in slow
motion, it tumbled to the ground.

"Ratso!" I yelled in despair as the bag
disappeared from sight behind the Big Wheel's
engine house.

Frantically we tore round the perimeter
fence. Scrambling over the boarding by the
engine house I dropped to the ground and
whirled round, expecting to see my rucksack
lying in a crumpled heap on the ground.

Bobby appeared beside me.

"Where is it?" he gasped.

I spun round again, searching the ground.

"It's not here!" I croaked. "Where is it?"

"I'm up here, pardner," I heard Ratso say.

We looked up in disbelief and I saw my rucksack hovering in the air above my head. Ratso's head was sticking out of the opening.

"Just as well I woke up, pardner," he said. "That could've ended up mighty nasty!"

I gaped at him.

"What are you doing up there?" I gurgled.
"Why – I mean – *how* are you doing that?"

"Hovering, you mean?"

"Yes."

"All *Wheeshes* can fly in times of emergency.
And that was sure one heck of an emergency,
wouldn't you say, pardner?"

"Are you OK, Ratso?" I asked as the bag
floated downwards into my arms.

"Sure. Another few metres and I'd have
been a goner, though," said the little alien.
"How in tarnation did I get up there?"

"Derek Butane did it," I said.

"The bully?" Ratso's eyes glittered. "That no-good son of a gun. I'll… I'll…"

"Easy, Ratso," I said, "don't excite yourself."

The little alien glowered.

"That boy's gettin' on my nerves," he said. "He'd better not cross my path again that's for sure. If he does there'll be trouble!"

I sighed. Trouble was something I was getting used to with Ratso around.

Chapter Seven

With Ratso perched on top of my rucksack Bobby and I left the Big Wheel and walked around the edge of the fun-fair. Just as we stepped on to the beach again we heard Naz Patel shout.

"Gary! Bobby! It's brilliant out here!"

We looked and saw him and Jonathan Brown waving to us from a small boat out in the bay. The rest of the class were out in boats too and Mr Anderton and Mrs Murphy sailed among them, keeping a watchful eye like the Admirals of the Fleet.

I waved back and spoke over my shoulder to Ratso.

"Time for your look at the sea," I said. "OK?"

The little alien shaded his eyes from the sun and looked at the boats.

"Okey-dokey, pardner," he replied. "Lead me to it."

Bobby and I hired a little boat at the jetty, put on our life jackets and five minutes later were out on the waves with the rest of the class.

Ratso looked over the side of the boat as Bobby rowed along.

"Really don't care for this sea stuff much," he drawled after a while. "It moves about a bit too much for my liking. Makes my stomach feel kinda funny."

"If you're going to be sick, Ratso," I said, "would you mind being sick over the side?"

"There's a bit of mist coming in," Bobby remarked. "Over there."

I looked towards the edge of the bay and saw what he meant. A white mist was creeping towards us from the sea.

"Might be an idea to get back to the jetty," I said. "We don't want to start rowing round in circles."

Suddenly there was a loud *thwack* on the side of our boat and we began to rock wildly.

"What—?" I cried. Twisting around I saw that another boat had come alongside and in it was Derek Butane and his two pals, Jimmy and Kev.

The Pain was standing up in the boat with an oar in his hand.

"Ha-haa!" he laughed. "What's wrong? Can't sail a little boat?" He gave our boat another blow with his oar and it tipped alarmingly.

"Cut that out!" yelled Bobby as we tried to keep our balance in the rocking boat.

"Doggone it!" shouted Ratso. "That guy has done it now. I'll… I'll…!" The little alien began to quiver with rage.

"No!" I yelped. "Please, don't!" I'd seen Ratso change shape when he was excited and I didn't want it to happen now.

The Pain thought I was talking to him.

"*Please*, Smithy? *Please*? Are you begging for mercy? Eh?" he grinned viciously. "Too bad!" he snarled. He swung the oar again… and missed.

"Aaargh!" With a surprised yelp he overbalanced, clawed at the air for a second, then fell overboard with a huge splash. His two pals looked over the edge of the boat in panic.

"Oi! Del!" yelled Jimmy. "You OK?"

"Of course he's OK," I snapped in annoyance. "He's got his life jacket on, hasn't he?"

"No!" cried Kev. "He took it off! Said it was poxy!"

"He can't swim!" yelled Jimmy. "He'll drown!"

"What?" I cried. I looked at The Pain and saw he was obviously having trouble staying afloat. He had drifted away from our two boats and was really floundering.

"Help!" he croaked, thrashing wildly. "Help!"

I grabbed an oar and stuck it out towards him.

"Grab this!" I yelled and at the same time heard Mr Anderton shout, "Hold on, Derek. I'm coming!"

Suddenly everything seemed to vanish. The sea mist had crept up unnoticed and covered us all in a thick white film. I could hardly see the end of the boat. The Pain was still shouting and splashing but in the echoing fog it was hard to tell where he was.

"What'll we do now?" said Bobby. "I know it's only The Pain, but we've got to help him."

"I know," I replied. I turned to Ratso. "Can you help, Ratso?" I asked. "Use your special powers?"

The little alien glared at me.

"Help that no-good son of a gun?" he spluttered in outrage. "Why should I?" He folded his arms and turned his back on me.

"Come on, Ratso," I wheedled. "I don't like him much either, but we can't just leave him to drown."

"Hmph!" grunted Ratso. "I suppose not." He climbed up on to the side of the boat and looked distastefully at the water. "I really don't like this sea stuff," he muttered. Then he took a deep breath, steadied himself and dived in.

Bobby and I stared over the edge of the boat as he disappeared below the surface with a small splash.

Two seconds later Ratso reappeared, spluttering and coughing. We could just make out his head above the water as the sea mist swirled around it. "I should've changed shape before I dived in," he croaked. "I'm not a very good swimmer." With that he disappeared beneath the waves again.

"Ratso!" I yelped. "Ratso!"

Just then the mist lifted a little and we saw Derek. He was still thrashing about and had drifted even further away into deeper water. He looked to be in big trouble.

"Help!" he shouted and thrashed some more.

It was then we all saw the shark's fin. It was cutting through the water – heading directly for Derek.

Derek saw it too and his eyes popped.

"Aaaah!" he screamed. He started to flail his arms even more but all he succeeded in doing was kicking up a lot of spray.

The shark bore down on him with terrifying speed. Just as it seemed as if it would open its jaws and swallow Derek, it slid beneath the waves.

The Pain twisted round in panic.

"Where'd it go?" he squealed. "Where'd it go?"

Suddenly, in a great spray of water, he was lifted out of the sea and began to rush towards us. Everyone gaped in astonishment as they realized that the shark had come up beneath him and that Derek was riding on its back.

Mr Anderton stared, his mouth hanging open in amazement.

"Cool!" exclaimed Bobby in wonder.

But Derek was not enjoying the ride. He had his eyes tightly shut and his hands clamped on the shark's fin.

"Aaaaah!" he moaned.

As the shark swept alongside our boat it suddenly slowed down and I realized it was our chance to save Derek.

"Come on!" I yelled at Bobby. "Let's get him!"

Both of us lunged forward, grabbed an arm each and hauled Derek out of the water. With hardly a ripple, the shark disappeared again beneath the waves. It was then I realized something about it. The shark had slowed down deliberately so we could save Derek. I dug Bobby in the ribs and grinned.

"The shark – it was Ratso!" I whispered.

Bobby stared then beamed. "Brilliant!" he said.

"What a rescue!" cried Mr Anderton. "Boys… you're heroes!"

"Not us, Mr Anderton," I murmured. "It's my rat that's the hero!"

Luckily the mist closed in again just long enough for Ratso to change back to normal and be lifted back on board. I dried him down with my towel as Bobby rowed us to the shore.

Ratso pointed to the shivering, miserable form of The Pain in the front of the boat.

"Looks like the baddie's been taken down a peg or two, pardner," he chortled and I grinned.

"It sure does," I whispered. "And I don't think he'll be bothering me again for a while. Thanks, Ratso."

The little alien smiled.

"No problem, pardner," he said. "Now, let's get on to dry land and have some fun."

"What have you got in mind?" I asked.

"Well, after all that excitement I think I can now see the point of just sittin' in the fun-fair riding nice and easy… goin' round and round and round…"

I grinned. "To the wooden horses, Ratso?"

"Yup! To the wooden horses, pardner," said Ratso. *"Yeeee-ha!"*

My Rat is ...

By Frank Rodgers

An exciting new Mega Stars series
Gary's rat is no ordinary pet.
Ratso is an alien from another planet.
An alien who's crash-landed in Gary's back garden...

Catch up with Ratso in these other stories:

My Rat is an Alien
Will Ratso be eaten by the local
moggies? And can Gary stop
anyone finding out about him?

My Rat is a Teacher
When Ratso comes to school, Gary
is worried – particularly when Derek
'The Pain' Butane is involved...

My Rat is a Cowboy
Ratso crash lands his spaceship on
a pony farm. Now he can be a *real*
cowboy. But one alien rat can
cause havoc on a horse...

For more information about Mega Stars, please contact:
The Sales Department, Macdonald Young Books,
61 Western Road, Hove, East Sussex BN3 1JD

Text and illustrations copyright © Frank Rodgers 1999

First published in Great Britain in 1999
by Macdonald Young Books
an imprint of Wayland Publishers Ltd
61 Western Road
Hove
East Sussex
BN3 1JD

Find Macdonald Young Books on the internet at
http://www.myb.co.uk

Designed by Don Martin
Printed and bound by Guernsey Press

British Library Cataloguing in Publication Data available

ISBN: 0 7500 2821 1

J111,588

£8.50